This igloo book belongs to:

....

igloobooks

Published in 2014
by Igloo Books Ltd
Cottage Farm
Sywell
NN6 0BJ
www.igloobooks.com

FIR003 0114
2 4 6 8 10 9 7 5 3 1
ISBN 978-1-78197-620-3

Illustrated by Gabriele Antonini

Printed and manufactured in China

Time for a Hug!

igloobooks

Snuggly Monster was a very cuddly monster.
He had soft fur and strong arms, perfect for giving warm,
lovable, fun, SQUEEZY, huggable hugs.

Snuggly loved to hug everyone he met.

He hugged
small **monsters.**

He hugged **tall**
ones.

He hugged sad monsters.

He hugged happy ones.

"Hugging is the best
fun in the world,"
thought Snuggly.

Then, one day, Snuggly was on his way to see his best friend, Giggly.
At the bus stop he met Stripy Monster.

Stripy's fur was dull and pale.
She was **very** cold from waiting for the bus.

Snuggly gave Stripy a **warm** hug and soon her fur was **bright** and **fluffy** again.

"Thanks, Snuggly!" she cried.

At last, the bus arrived and Snuggly got on.
He saw Noisy Monster looking sad.
"I've lost my voice," said Noisy, in a tiny whisper.

Snuggly gave Noisy a hug to cheer him up.
Noisy was so pleased he forgot that he was sad.
"Thank you, Snuggly," he whispered.

At the next stop, Snuggly heard a strange noise.
He saw little Bouncy Monster on the road.

He'd **bounced** into
a lamp post and **bumped** his knee.

Snuggly jumped off the bus,
scooped Bouncy up and gave him a hug.
Bouncy stopped crying right away.

Snuggly's hug made his knee stop hurting,
just like magic.

At last, Snuggly arrived at Giggly's house.
He couldn't wait to give his friend a hug.
He pressed the doorbell,

((ding-dong,))
((ding-dong.))

Snuggly waited and waited, but no one answered the door.

Suddenly, Snuggly heard giggling sounds
coming from the back garden.

He p^{ee}ped

over the fence

and saw his best friend Giggly playing
with someone new!

Giggly and the someone new

swung on the swing.

Then, they slid down the slide.

Suddenly, Snuggly felt sad.
"Giggly has forgotten all about me,"
he said with a sniffle.

Then, Snuggly saw the someone new give Giggly Monster a

great, big hug.

Snuggly's happiness vanished and **BIG,** watery tears dribbled down his face and onto his fur.

"Giggly monster's got a new best friend!"

he wailed.

Snuggly **sobbed** and **sobbed.**

More tears came,
drip, drop, plip, plop.

Snuggly Monster made such a noise that Stripy,
Bouncy and Noisy came running.
"What's the matter?" they asked.

Just then, Giggly and the someone new
came out of the garden.

They wanted to know
why Snuggly Monster
was crying, too.

Snuggly Monster pointed at the someone new and said,
"Giggly's got a new best friend!"

Then, Snuggly Monster started crying all over again.
Big, fat tears
splashed into puddles on the ground.

Giggly explained that the someone new was his cousin,
Funny Monster. "You're my only best friend, Snuggly," he said.

Snuggly Monster had made a mistake and he
felt very silly indeed.
"I'm sorry, Funny," he said.

"I'm sorry, Giggly and Stripy and Noisy and Bouncy."

"Never mind," said Giggly, "Everyone makes mistakes.
What you need now, Snuggly,

is a great, big hug!"

All the monsters gathered round and gave
Snuggly Monster the

biggest, huggiest hug

he'd **ever** had.

"That was LOVELY!" said Snuggly Monster.
All his tears dried up and suddenly
he felt **happy** again.

"Come on everyone," said Giggly,
"let's all play in the garden."

The monsters had fun all afternoon playing lots of games and Snuggly was back to his old self.

He gave everyone lots of hugs

and he felt **happier** than ever.

That night, Snuggly Monster cuddled up in bed with his teddy.
He remembered the lovely hug from all his monster friends.

"I love giving hugs, but I **love** getting them, too."
thought Snuggly.

Then, he settled down to a
lovely, huggily, snuggily sleep.